Historical Disasters

Chernobyl

by Julie Murray

Dash!
LEVELED READERS
An Imprint of Abdo Zoom • abdobooks.com

Dash!
LEVELED READERS

Level 1 – Beginning
Short and simple sentences with familiar words or patterns for children who are beginning to understand how letters and sounds go together.

Level 2 – Emerging
Longer words and sentences with more complex language patterns for readers who are practicing common words and letter sounds.

Level 3 – Transitional
More developed language and vocabulary for readers who are becoming more independent.

THIS BOOK CONTAINS RECYCLED MATERIALS

abdobooks.com

Published by Abdo Zoom, a division of ABDO, PO Box 398166, Minneapolis, Minnesota 55439.

Printed in the United States of America, North Mankato, Minnesota.
052023
092023

Photo Credits: Getty Images, Science Source, Shutterstock
Production Contributors: Kenny Abdo, Jennie Forsberg, Grace Hansen, John Hansen
Design Contributors: Candice Keimig, Neil Klinepier

Library of Congress Control Number: 2022947147

Publisher's Cataloging in Publication Data

Names: Murray, Julie, author.
Title: Chernobyl / by Julie Murray
Description: Minneapolis, Minnesota : Abdo Zoom, 2024 | Series: Historical disasters | Includes online resources and index.
Identifiers: ISBN 9781098281212 (lib. bdg.) | ISBN 9781098281915 (ebook) | ISBN 9781098282264 (Read-to-me ebook)
Subjects: LCSH: Disasters--Juvenile literature. | History--Juvenile literature. | Chernobyl Nuclear Accident, Chornobyl', Ukraine, 1986--Juvenile literature.
Classification: DDC 363.17--dc23

Table of Contents

Chernobyl

The Chernobyl nuclear power **plant** in Ukraine is the site of the worst nuclear disaster in history.

Правик
Кургуз
ИГНАТЕНКО
ОРЛОВ

In the initial explosion, two workers were killed. Within a few months, 28 more were dead. Thousands became sick from the **radiation**. Some died years later.

April 26, 1986

The disaster began early in the morning on April 26, 1986. Workers were doing a safety test on a **reactor**. A power surge caused several explosions. A fire quickly followed.

The **plant** began leaking **radiation** into the air. The levels were 100 times greater than what was safe. The wind carried the radiation over many areas throughout Europe.

The city of Pripyat was just two miles (3 km) from the **plant**. It had a population of 50,000. They all were exposed to dangerous levels of **radiation**.

Plants, animals, and farmland were also **contaminated**. A forest close to the site was named the "Red Forest." The trees there died and turned reddish-orange in color.

The Clean Up

Thousands of workers were sent to clean up the site. Most of them did not have proper protection. Many of them became very sick.

A giant steel shell was built around the site to prevent more **radiation** from leaking out. Still, no one was allowed to live within a 20-mile (32-km) radius of the site.

Today, the area is still highly **contaminated**. Scientists can enter for a limited amount of time. They believe it may take up to 20,000 years for the area to be safe again!

More Facts

- The Chernobyl disaster was covered up until Sweden demanded answers. The country detected high levels of **radiation** that had traveled with the wind.
- Scientists estimate that 4,000 to 200,000 people will eventually die from the accident. This is due to their radiation exposure.
- Farm animals were born deformed after the incident. Many people suffered for years with health problems such as cancer.

Glossary

contaminated – made dirty or unusable by adding something to it.

plant – a building or group of buildings that have machinery and equipment for making things.

radiation – the waves of energy sent out by sources of heat or light, or by radioactive material. Exposure to high levels of ionizing radiation in a short period of time can cause serious illness and death.

reactor – a device in physics for starting and controlling a nuclear chain reaction.

Index

Online Resources

Booklinks
NONFICTION NETWORK
FREE! ONLINE NONFICTION RESOURCES

To learn more about Chernobyl, please visit **abdobooklinks.com** or scan this QR code. These links are routinely monitored and updated to provide the most current information available.